Katherine Caine

Light on the hidden way

Katherine Caine

Light on the hidden way

ISBN/EAN: 9783337270322

Printed in Europe, USA, Canada, Australia, Japan

Cover: Foto ©Andreas Hilbeck / pixelio.de

More available books at **www.hansebooks.com**

LIGHT ON THE HIDDEN WAY

With an Introduction

BY

JAMES FREEMAN CLARKE

Heaven doth with us as we with torches do,
Not light them for themselves; for if our virtues
Did not go forth of us, 't were all alike
As if we had them not. Spirits are not finely touched
But to fine issues.

SHAKSPEARE.

BOSTON
TICKNOR AND COMPANY
1886

DEDICATION.

To the Sorrowing, Life-weary, and Sin-laden; to all who may find in these pages "that cup of strength in some great agony,"—

This little Book is Enscribed,

with an earnest trust that, though it contain great potency for pain, its deeper message is one of inspiration, strength, comfort, and that Peace of God which passeth all understanding.

INTRODUCTION.

THE following remarkable story of a personal experience is written by a lady who is herself firmly persuaded of its reality. I feel bound to testify that the writer is regarded by many intelligent and cultivated men and women, who are her personal friends, as sincere, truthful, and conscientious. I will add that she has had no connection with so-called "Spiritualism," and is unacquainted with any of the professional mediums. Her report, therefore, is an independent one, and deserves attention from those engaged in investigating this occult Borderland, where beings of the other world are reported as coming into relations with the inhabitants of our own. According to the view of this writer, those who thus present themselves may often be in a low state, having missed their way upward and needing advice and encouragement from those still in the body. The moral tone and influence of this little book cannot but be useful even to those who are not prepared either to accept or reject its conclusions.

JAMES FREEMAN CLARKE.

JANUARY 1, 1886.

Lo, at length the True Light! Light for every man born into the world, kindling the faces of them that receive it, till they become the children of God!

Cease, blinding glories of the heavens, which none could see and live!

Cease, gross darkness of the earth, where the righteous put forth their hands and fear!

The veil between is taken away, and the mingling dayspring comes.

No longer is the dwelling of Eternal Life too bright above, and the perishable world too dark below. No more strangers and exiles, but fellow-citizens with the saints and of the household of God. For Thou hast made one family, there and here, one living communion of seen and unseen. We had said, "Thou layest men fast in everlasting sleep;" but lo, they sleep into everlasting waking!

Blessed be the Eternal, who giveth beauty for ashes, and the garment of praise for the spirit of heaviness!

LIGHT ON THE HIDDEN WAY.

My dear Friend, — You ask me why I do not tell you more of myself, and let you keep near to my inner life. Perhaps your question is the key to my long silences, for I cannot write superficially to you, and it is not easy to speak, much less to write, out of the depths.

But since our separation is likely to be a permanent one, I will try to live in the spirit with you, and in the future to give you at least some glimpses of my deeper experiences.

Again, you tell me that my letters "hint of some rare gift," reminding you of strange sayings in my childhood. Is it so? Beginning now to realize that I am in a way unlike those about me, I speak less spontaneously, though not without an inward protest. "Quench not the spirit" continually reproaches me when I am silent, and yet would so gladly speak the word of assurance and comfort.

It seems strange to me that those who profess to believe in the immortal life, and to treasure the Bible, where angels ascending and descending hold familiar converse with men, and who though believing in the transfiguration and resurrection of Jesus, are so averse to the idea of a continued communication between the two worlds, and receive with coldness and unfaith the assurance that the friend called dead stands beside them most keenly alive. Thus I have learned silence. But for how long? I wait the growth of this wonder-seed. Something whispers to me that it shall bear precious fruit, from which may be distilled drops of healing for the sin-sick and sorrowing. How grateful I am that I have you to wait and watch with me!

I have read of late many scientific books, but meet with nothing that will in any way account for what comes to me. Dr. Carpenter's "unconscious cerebration" is to my mind insufficient and unsatisfactory; but among the spiritual gifts enumerated by Saint Paul we find that of *sight*, and his simple recognition of it as a spiritual faculty seems both natural and reasonable.

You ask what I know of Spiritualism. Nothing whatever from my own experience, never having seen a public medium or read any Spiritualistic literature, as I have wished my mind unbiassed by their views. The little I have heard through friends is distasteful to me. I am reluctant to believe that one can command the presence of a number of unknown spirits, or that such intercourse could be any gratification to earnest souls. "The spirit bloweth where it listeth;" and these experiences come to me or are withheld, "not as I will."

That Spiritualism, in its purest and highest sense, is God's new dispensation to mankind, I do believe; and though tares are springing up with the wheat, a goodly harvest will in time be realized for the spiritual needs of the world. Are we not ready for it? Our best teaching is pregnant with this prophecy; and the world of thought, like the earth in these spring-days, seems quivering with expectancy, thrilled with the consciousness of a growth which may burst into a flood of blossom while we watch.

You know how busy my girlhood was. My days continue to be filled to overflowing with practical duties, moments for reading being snatched from the common round of many cares.

I cannot think of this "open vision" as in the least unnatural, it is so a part of my daily life, — a glowing thread of light interwoven with its sombre tones. Very often, when with friends or strangers, I see their dear ones with them, frequently those whom I have not known in this life. For instance, this afternoon, while sitting with a friend, I saw upon her knee the little girl whom she has lost, caressing her unconscious mother most tenderly.

I spoke of the child, and of the comfort in the thought that our dead are often with us; but she, poor soul, shrank from this idea. She would not like to feel that a disembodied spirit was near her, it would give her no pleasure, but make her nervous. She rather clung to the belief in a future resurrection day; but if it were true that death is only the portal to the higher life, even then she could not believe the dead were near the earth, but in that happy land, far, far away. And so I feel as if walking with those born blind, who cannot comprehend the beauty of sunshine and sweet faces.

And yet I know that others have this gift, although it would seem to be rare. My father had it in a less degree, and my brother sees, but does not hear. We frequently see the same spirit simultaneously.

I have not answered your question, "How do they look to you? Like ghostly shadows?" Not at all; and yet their conditions are so various, one might as easily describe in one term what flowers with their infinite variety of color and texture look like. Some appear as if still in the flesh, so that I have sometimes been puzzled; others appear to have become deformed, or almost animal; and then there are those with shining garments and an atmosphere that suggests cathedral music and sunshine streaming through stained glass. I usually see the light or atmosphere first, — sometimes faint or cloudy, and occasionally overpoweringly bright and beautiful.

Clothes? Yes. Some seem still to cling to the latest fashions, while the more spiritual are clad in flowing robes of light of various hues and degrees of purity.

. . . .

You know that this gift dates back to my earliest recollections. My mother left me when a baby, and yet I have always known her face. I remember once, when quite a little child, following her, as I thought; and when she disappeared, not understanding, I ran, thinking to overtake her, till quite exhausted. I thought she lived in the moon, and I always felt safe and happy in the moonlight, because, I understand now, her spiritual atmosphere is like moonlight. I often wake to find her sitting by my bedside, and when I am in pain or trouble she is much with me. Once she reproved me for my mood, and bade me read a poem, telling me what book to find it in, the page and author. I had never seen or heard of it; but it was there, just what I needed.

I feel as if my father's eyes were always upon me. When I was about ten years old I had set my room in order one Saturday morning, and being in haste to get out, had swept around the rug, and dusted in like manner. As I started to go, I saw my father standing on the rug, looking down on it intently. Raising his solemn eyes to mine, he told me to lift one end of it.

I have never forgotten my mortification, or his charge to remember that no act or thought is hidden, and that every slighted duty is a sin against the ideal life.

It was years before it occurred to me that every one had not this same vision. Ghost-stories did not affect my thought of heavenly any more than of earthly friends. Indeed I did not connect the idea with them, but supposed it referred to the rising and reanimation of the dead body, — which appeared to me as reasonable as to hear that a dress had come out of a trunk and gone about to frighten people.

I just remember taking tea at a neighbor's, and when I said good-night, being asked if I was afraid to go home alone. Confident that I was not, I started; but finding it blustering, dark, and lonely, I soon became timid and uncertain of my way. Presently I discovered a little light beside me, and then, in the light, the baby who had gone the year before. He kept just before me till I opened the front door, and then, with the sweetest smile, was gone.

At the funeral of one I loved, I saw him beside his mother and sisters, and wondered that their grief seemed to prevent them from seeing him. When the casket was laid away, the vault seemed full of light and flowers.

I have no recollection of ever feeling fear, and surprise came as the knowledge gradually dawned upon me that my sight was something unusual. . . .

Some time since, I was passing a church with a friend as the members were assembling for the funeral of their pastor.

Following an impulse, we too went in. Presently the *cortège* arrived, the good rector himself preceding the mourners in their slow and solemn tread through the aisle and remaining at the head of the casket during the service. We followed the congregation into the churchyard, to find the reverend gentleman again, bending pathetically over his sobbing widow beside his own grave. As there had been a double congregation in the church, so at the grave a chorus of heavenly voices swelled the parting hymn into what seemed a song of rejoicing and welcome to the new-comer, while voices and faces gradually disappeared in the glory of light.

I have a great love for churches, and seldom find one empty. When visiting in R——, I went into an old church; and while examining a tablet, saw for a moment the form of a young girl beside it. A few days later, while calling upon a lady with whom I was slightly acquainted, I noticed hanging over the piano a colored photograph, which I recognized unmistakably as a picture of the face I had seen in the church. This proved to be a likeness of the lady's daughter, and a near relative also of the friend who had called my attention to the tablet.

One evening I attended service in a little church belonging to a sect almost unknown and quite unpopular here. The congregation was small, but there was more spirit and earnestness in their worship than is often seen in larger assemblies. During the prayer three figures appeared below the arched ceiling bending over the worshippers, — one a woman, and two suggested old pictures of the Patriarchs. Presently another and more radiant form joined them, and pausing, looked up in an expectant attitude. The white light grew more and more brilliant, until a shining one in an intensity of light, with long, wonderful wings,[1] was just visible within it, when the expectant figure raised his hand, as if to stay the dazzling glory. The tableau, as it were, remained thus, the ineffable light streaming over the hushed worshippers until the close of the prayer.

Speaking of churches, do you never feel there is something more than the stillness and association of the place that makes it to many of us "none other than the house of God and the gate of heaven?" I believe

[1] I have seldom seen wings, but have been told that they are symbolic of a very high degree of spirituality.

I could write a volume on what I have seen and heard in them. Sometimes the altar is beautifully decked with flowers and the air filled with exquisite music. I have been almost spell-bound by the deep volume of sound during the singing of a congregational hymn when only a handful of rainy-day saints were present in the pews.

Have I told you of the white light, so wonderful in its intensity? Occasionally it fills the church, but more frequently descends upon individuals. Indeed, the seeking, prayerful soul is recognized in this way, though personally unknown to me. This ineffable light always comes with more or less intensity in response to sincere prayer, and I doubt not is the means by which comfort and strength are borne in upon the soul. Light! how freighted with meaning is that word,—purifying, strengthening, quickening, illuminating!

Some day I think we shall care more for symbols, using them rationally for their spiritual signification, without superstition. I should be glad to see the *ever-burning* lamp swung in our churches and in every home,—symbol of the aspiring flame of the soul and the light which continually streams from the Father, "who covereth himself with light as with a garment."

Is the repeated dwelling by sacred writers upon the white light merely imagination and coincidence? "The white light proceeding from the great white throne," the New Jerusalem, which "has no need of the sun, neither of the moon, for the glory of God does lighten it," and in the transfiguration, the garments "white as no fuller on earth could white them," for "*as he prayed*, the fashion of his countenance was altered, and his raiment was white and glistering." "And behold, there talked with him two men, which were Moses and Elias, who appeared in glory." Was it indeed only a sunstroke, that light from heaven which blinded Paul and smote him to the earth as he journeyed toward Damascus, so searching his conscience that it revolutionized the whole tenor of his work and life?

. . . .

Your question, "How do they speak to you? Give me an idea of your intercourse with them," is strangely difficult to answer.

In the first place, let me say that I am convinced this gift is a spiritual faculty, entirely independent of the physical senses; for darkness or sunlight, the roar of the city streets or the stillness of my chamber, are alike immaterial conditions. Nor is it only those who have laid aside the earthly tabernacle that are thus unveiled to my sight. Frequently, where I have felt indifference, even prejudice, I have been touched and rebuked by the unexpected loveliness of the inner man or woman, and as often shocked to find those I should like to respect, dark and repulsive.

. . . .

The impossibility of imparting to another the quickening glow we receive from finer souls, will prevent my giving you more than a very imperfect rendering of the teachings I have received. But this is the substance of a conversation held with my father this evening. I had just left the piano, after playing "Coronation," and was enjoying the sunset from the bay-window, feeling unusually bright and peaceful. Standing beside me, he said: "You are happy to-night, because the day has been calm and restful; nothing has occurred to disturb its peace. You have not been good, any more than you were in your sleep last night; you have rested. Should to-morrow be a day of trial, shall I find you at evening conquered, or conqueror? Will you have kept this peace in your heart undisturbed? Will you have listened to harshness and injustice in silence and without anger, returning a kind answer? Will you have been patient and cheerful in sacrificing yourself to others, remembering their faults tenderly, your own seriously? Will you have kept your thoughts above littleness and your soul open to the inflowing spirit? Should you succeed in doing this, you will feel a far deeper peace than this mere rest from spiritual labor."

"I know," I replied, "but I could not do all that if my life depended on it."

"Your life does depend on it; your whole future life depends on just that, — whether or not you slay the dragon self. It will be a long struggle, but you can and must do it, or else fail utterly in your life work."

"What is my life work?" I asked.

"It is first to conquer yourself; then to develop and use wisely your physical, intellectual, and spiritual being. Do this, and you will find your sphere of influence widening, your five talents become ten. You have enough to do now, rather more than you have yet been equal to, in your own heart and home. Recognizing your pain and loneliness, I come, to help you if I can, and keep you from discouragement and failure; to inspire you to rise above it all and save you from bitterness and unsanctified sorrow. We feel the deepest sympathy with you. It is a dreary life, hedged in with briers and thorns. Yes, dear, but look up. The sky is as blue, the stars shine as brightly and solemnly for you, as for those upon the sunny slopes of happiness. Hold your dull life up to the light and see how it will be transfigured. Life is not meant to be a path of ease, but steep and rugged; and it is only through self-denial, discouragement, discipline, and trial that you may attain the higher life.

"Believe me, you can no more develop the spiritual powers without use and exercise than you can the physical. There is no virtue in being patient, if your patience is never tried; cheerful, if you are not tempted to be gloomy. It is the little words you speak, the little thought you think, the little thing you do or leave undone, the little moments you waste or use wisely, the little temptations which you yield to or overcome, — the *little* things of every day that are making or marring your future life.

"Of course you will fail sometimes; but see to it that you rise from every fall with a renewed spirit and stronger will, determined to win a blessing from every foe.

Be peaceful and joyous; consecrate the simplest duties of every day; fill your life with earnest endeavor and perfect trust: and no matter how narrow and painful it may seem to you, when it is ended you will look back with wonder at the influence for good your quiet example and cheerful spirit have been, and realize also that you have won no small victory; while in failing to reach your possibilities you injure others. Remember there is no legacy like the example of a holy life."

. . . .

While busy in my room, to-night, there came to me a venerable man, a beautiful presence. He greeted me and said: —

"You are rarely gifted. You hold a solemn trust, a light that should glorify your life. Do you value it as you should? Do you realize what failure means here, — remorse, regret, and sorrow for lost opportunities; words and acts your agony cannot recall; neglect too late to repair? So subtle is the far-reaching influence of a life, that not only must you meet your own failure and its influence upon those about you, but often, for generations, face the effect of the good or evil you did or left undone. This is judgment.

"There are some poor souls who go through life without learning a conscious lesson. Inherited tendencies, a lack of moral training, cruel circumstances, and all manner of chilling influences would seem to have utterly blasted their spiritual natures. Yet the germ of good is there, dormant in its dull husk, and here, shall be quickened into life. You know there are some seeds that will not germinate in the cold, open ground of northern latitudes, and that it is only in a more genial atmosphere that they can be made to unfold. Sometimes it happens so with this germ soul; and here, in the Divine Nursery, not a seed is lost, but all wake to new possibilities.

"The first thrill of life may be a terrible agony of remorse,—the painful bursting of the hull. Then, for the first time, perhaps, comes to it a consciousness of what it is and what it might have been. A reaction from the belief in a literal hell has given many the very comfortable idea, that no matter how selfishly and unworthily they may have lived, at death their sins will be blotted out,—that *then* they will begin to live better lives and enter into joy and peace. Nothing could be farther from the truth. If a child play with matches and is burned, the loving mother will nurse him tenderly and teach him that his suffering is the consequence of his disobedience. Do all she can to soothe and heal, the lesson must be learned.

"Thus, if the children of the all-wise, all-loving Parent disobey his laws, the suffering must follow. You will enter this life just what you make yourself. If you allow your spirit to be cramped, dwarfed, and sin-stained, you will find yourself crippled, weak, and impure; unfit for the companionship of the good, and unable to enjoy the spiritual life until you have atoned by long struggle. If you persistently resist temptation and hurtful shadows, and keep your soul receptive to all purifying, inspiring influences, your fitness to receive them will increase, and you will enter here prepared for higher development and purer joys."

. . . .

Talking with my father this morning, I asked him about Spiritualism. He said:

"The so-called Spiritualist has no conception of pure spirituality. Instead of spiritualizing the present, he would materialize the future, placing it upon his level instead of reverently striving to rise to ours. There is also a loss of the sense of the Divine Presence — the highest and purest communion. He is apt to be less conscientious than those who feel less assurance, and utterly fails to realize the responsibility of life; while each day brings him nearer its close, without realizing how it will be with him when all that is material has vanished. Be sure that he will stand on the threshold of Eternity shivering, for he will have failed to weave his spiritual garment.

"The true Spiritualist is one whose life is sanctified by the Spirit,—a perpetual consecration. You have Jesus for your Ideal. He said, 'I sanctify myself,' so perfect was his consecration. After his death, when his disciples were assembled at the familiar meal, so fraught with tender associations, he appeared in their midst,—not to hold a séance, to lift the table, or tell them of the life to come, but simply to impress his teachings upon them and fill their hearts with peace; to breathe upon them his holy spirit and charge them to be faithful to the light they had received. Nor do you find them waiting in the dark for him to come again, but working, through trial and persecution, to advance the coming of his kingdom. This is the only true Spiritualism."

. . . .

Speaking of a friend to her father, he said: "I regret her want of health, but she must strive to overcome it, so far as lies in her power, by the might of the spirit. Better spend herself in work than rust away. Remember, it is claimed that a knowledge of the future life tends to the neglect of daily duties. Let every detail of your work be done as reverently and conscientiously as if arranging the tiny stones in a delicate mosaic, — a part of the Master's temple."

"But her life is so distasteful," I pleaded.

"If her life is distasteful to her, it is a sin that she allows it to be so, for since it is the work now given her, she should do it with the utmost earnestness and consecration. An example that will teach her children the holiness of labor and the sinfulness of wasted time will be the most precious legacy she can leave them. A faith that can make weary, struggling souls faithful in the least of things, that consecrates the whole of life; a faith lived rather than spoken, filling the soul with 'joy and peace in believing,'—must win the world. If our presence and sympathy make you live better lives and hold you up to higher spiritual aims, you need no words to prove it. That is the only test you require."

. . . .

Thank you for your dear letter of sympathy. If I feel my arms so empty and my heart and home so desolate, how must it be with those who sit in darkness!

As the little spirit breathed softly away, a strange calm came over me. I seemed blinded by the light and sense of awe and mystery. I saw and felt my mother take the little fellow from my arms; and startled to a sudden sense of resistance, found that I held only the empty shell, "out of which the pearl had gone."

The day passed without a glimmer from beyond; but in the sleepless night, so painfully free from care, my father stood by my bedside holding my darling in his arms. It was only for a moment; but I was comforted. We laid the little casket away in a driving northeast storm.

Oh, how it moaned and beat upon my heart!

I tried to live my faith, and accept my loneliness as his gain, and trust that in God's providence it shall be mine also.

A friend brought me this exquisite little poem by Mrs. Lowell, which I copy for you, as you may not have seen it. It has comforted me to repeat it, especially, as the closing verses recall the night I saw my father holding my little lamb.

TO A FRIEND AFTER THE LOSS OF A CHILD.

MRS. JAMES RUSSELL LOWELL.

When on my ear your loss was knelled,
And tender sympathy upburst,
A little spring from memory welled
Which once had quenched my bitter thirst;

And I was fain to bear to you
  A portion of its mild relief,
That it might be as cooling dew
  To steal some fever from your grief.

After our child's untroubled breath
  Up to the Father took its way,
And on our home the shade of death
  Like a long twilight haunting lay,

And friends came round with us to weep
  The little spirit's swift remove, —
This story of the Alpine sheep
  Was told to us by one we love.

They, in the valley's sheltering care,
  Soon crop their meadow's tender prime;
And when the sod grows brown and bare,
  The shepherd strives to make them climb

To any shelves of pasture green
  That hang along the mountain side,
Where grass and flowers together lean,
  And down through mists the sunbeams glide.

But nought can lure the timid things
  The steep and rugged path to try,
Though sweet the shepherd call and sing,
  And seared below the pastures lie, —

Till in his arms their lambs he takes,
  Along the dizzy verge to go ;
When, heedless of the rifts and breaks,
  They follow on o'er rock and snow.

And in those pastures lifted fair,
  More dewy soft than lowland mead,
The shepherd drops his tender care,
  And sheep and lambs together feed.

This parable, by Nature breathed,
  Blew on me as the south wind free
O'er frozen brooks that float unsheathed
  From icy thraldom to the sea.

A blissful vision through the night
  Would all my happy senses sway,
Of the Good Shepherd on the height,
  Or climbing up the starry way,

Holding our little lamb asleep,
And, like the burden of the sea,
Sounding that voice along the deep,
Saying, "Arise, and follow me!"

Since that last vision I have seemed to be left in darkness. Why, I cannot say. Possibly my own intensity of feeling is the barrier, or it may be a needed discipline. And yet, how much more comfort and assurance have I, than others who are suffering the same heartache? I feel doubly bereft; for not only has the child gone, but the gates through which he entered seem to have closed upon him. There is a reason for it, though I may not understand, and I will be patient. It may be my soul's winter, and the spring will come again with re-awakened blossoms.

. . . .

You ask if my faith has made my sorrow easier to bear. Yes, it must be so; because I know that it is well with the child.

"In that great cloister's stillness and seclusion,
By guardian angels led,
Safe from temptation, safe from sin's pollution,
He lives whom we call dead."

But though I believe this, sometimes I feel that could we only have known how to keep him he might have been a helper in the world's work. The thought so beautifully expressed in the following lines by Julia C. R. Dorr makes me at times unreconciled.

"Thy brothers, they are mortal, they must tread
Ofttimes in rough, hard ways, with bleeding feet;
Must fight with dragons, must bewail their dead,
And fierce Apollyon face to face must meet.

Was God, then, kinder unto thee than them,
  O thou whose little life was but a span?
Ah, think it not! In all his diadem
  No star shines brighter than the kingly man

Who nobly earns whatever crown he wears,
  Who grandly conquers, or as grandly dies,
And the white banner of his manhood bears
  Through all the years uplifted to the skies!

What lofty pæans shall the victor greet!
  What crown resplendent for his brow be fit!
O child, if earthly life be bitter-sweet,
  Hast thou not something missed in missing it?"

That passive resignation which accepts everything as the will of God is no longer possible to me; the question continually arises, as to how much misery is God's will, and how much the consequence of our ignorance and blindness. For instance, when loved members of a family die from the neglect of common sanitary measures, does not the destroyer come into our homes as the penalty of broken laws, whether broken through wilful blindness or ignorance? and is it not irreverent to say it is God's will that we suffer? When ship or railroad train, freighted with precious lives, is swept away through the careless-ness of officials, or may be the incompe-tence of just one man, is it providential? or are not these things allowed rather be-cause God's laws are immutable, and we only learn to adjust ourselves to them by these solemn lessons?

It does seem hard that the innocent should suffer. In this sense we are surely members one of another, — if one member suffer, all members suffer with it; but as humanity learns the Divine lesson of in-dividual responsibility, will not these laws, at first sight so cruel, come to be recognized as wise and beneficent, because fixed and unchangeable?

One spar I hold fast to on this dark sea of questioning, — a faith, growing out of every day's experience, as well as by tracing the ways of the Spirit in history, in an overruling Providence which evolves good out of evil, light from darkness, life out of death, and makes "the fairest flowers spring from old dead decay." Longing and questioning will arise; but in my best moods I feel that if the child went through some ignorance of mine, even then, that heavenly life is full of compensation to him, and through the discipline of sorrow, loneliness, yes, even doubt, may come to me a blessed spiritual growth, otherwise impossible.

I have seen and heard very little the past

months, just enough to know they are still about me. Perhaps the waters of my soul are too ruffled to reflect my heavenly lights. The other day, I had this interesting experience. Sitting in the sunshine with my book, the child of a friend stood beside me. He often visits me, though I never saw him in this life. We spoke of his mother and my baby; and stroking his lovely hair, I said, "I wish I could send your mamma a curl!" So seized was I with the idea that, rising, I went to my work-table for a pair of scissors, and coming back to the child, selected a curl to cut. As the scissors touched the hair, he dropped his eyes with such an amused, quizzical smile, and laughed outright at my look of dismay that the curl did not come. "Did you really think you could cut it?" he asked.

[A number of the succeeding letters have been omitted.]

I have been, and am still, groping through great doubt and gloom. How will it end? Shall I find my way out with a stronger faith, or are all my old stays giving way under me? I doubt everything now. Even the sunshine seems changed, the joy to have gone out of everything. All my life I have accepted things as they came to me, and formed through reading and experience certain opinions; but now have come to the time when my house is shaken to its foundations by the storms and floods that will assail us, if we think. I only know that I want *truth* at any cost, and all I have held most precious must go, if not built upon "a foundation that standeth sure." You ask if I have been reading Herbert Spencer and the "Index." Yes, and a good deal besides; for I believe that not knowledge, but a *little* knowledge, is a dangerous thing.

This evening I was sitting on the piazza, watching the close of a perfect April day. Early there had been a cloudless sky and calm, still waters, changing to wild, black squalls of rain and wind, with bursts of gladsome sunlight in between; and now all clouds had fled, and the sun was setting as peacefully as it had risen, shedding its rosy hue over the placid river. Restless and gloomy, the peace of the hour seemed almost a mockery; for I was far more in sympathy with the dull sky and stormy waters.

A hand was laid on my shoulder; and turning my head, I saw my father. He did not speak for some time, but at length said: —

"Do you know it is not necessary to die to descend into hell and to feel its despair and misery? To look at life and the future as you do, is to descend step by step into torment. To use your reason is right and necessary; but you are now unreasonable, and rejecting the light. I warn you that if you persist in shutting it out, you will lose it.

"You are aware of the great diversity of gifts; that to some have been given ten talents, while others have received but one. Will you dare decide how much value yours may be to the Master, and bury it in the ground? This moment you are doubting if I am really here, or whether there is something the matter with your brain.

You see and hear me, you are conscious of the pressure of my hand. Can you not understand that all are not equally gifted? that some gifts are exceptional? If you possess this in an unusual degree, is not that all the more reason for valuing it? You have no idea how it may develop, under the influence of a firm conviction and sunny faith, to be of blessed strength and comfort to many."

. . . .

Your efforts to cheer me are very kind. I am not gloomy from any physical cause, and a change of scene would not divert me. One cannot run away from oneself.

Still the same questioning? Yes; and is it not strange, *if* this spiritual intercourse is an hallucination, that I find it so difficult to accept it? and also that when my doubt is the gravest, I cannot separate my thought of the future from what I know of it through these experiences? Still, that may be a part of the delusion; just as we can think out both sides of an argument and connect with one idea all we have associated with it.

You say you do not see why, in giving this up, I should lose faith in everything. Nor do I, except that the entire experience of my life seems so intimately connected with it. I think, in those half unconscious depths of the soul, I still believe in God and his providential guidance, and in the reality of that other world and all I have seen and heard; and yet the surface waters are so disturbed I can no longer think of it without pain, while worship has long since been impossible to me. The universe seems like a vast machine, — iron, pitiless, — and we, grinding through our existence, the victims of the machine; our affections the oil that keeps us from self-destruction. With all our boasted knowledge, we really know so little of the laws that control the blending of matter and spirit that it seems hopeless to satisfy the reason. And what is intuition, but perhaps a mild form of my disease? My deepest pain is in the thought that I have awakened a false hope in those who have loved and trusted me. They are aware of all my misgivings; yet it is impossible for me to shake their faith. Fortunately they are few in number, for it has been too sacred and intimate a part of my life to be spoken, except to those very near me. Poor dear hearts! When I thought to give them bread, did I give them a stone? Your sympathy and interest are most grateful to me. When I catch a gleam of light, you shall share it.

. . . .

My dear father, if he be a fact, is most patient with me. My imperfect notes of his talks with me can give you little idea of the force of his spoken words, or the impressiveness of his manner. He greeted me this afternoon in this wise: —

"So you are still in the fog, dear. Perhaps I can let in a ray of sunshine. We will suppose that I am a myth, and if there be a future life, that it is infinitely distant, where the redeemed, dead to all love and longing, all disinterested devotion, are content to sing eternal hallels, unmindful of those who have been their joy and care. You know you cannot believe in such a heaven as this, that it is inconsistent with the higher conceptions of God and progress. Then why not accept the one which appeals to your reason and conscience? Or if your present life is all, if its high aims and aspirations are merely the fragrance of a passing flower, what, then, will it matter that you have had this comfort and cheer?

"No, of course you do not wish to be a victim to a self-delusion through some reaction of your own brain; but you are no more able to satisfy yourself of this than of the reality of your spiritual perception. 'Spiritual things are spiritually discerned,' and can never be demonstrated to your satisfaction except through an act of faith. For months you have lived without faith, persistently rejecting a natural, useful faculty. Have you been happier? Have you been inspired with a greater earnestness and enthusiasm? Or has your soul been bound to a treadmill, — the angel within you grown dull and sad?

"I think you must decide which is the reasonable, rational, and most reverent faith, and having decided, hold to it; for you surely cannot think that you will not be held accountable for the way you use this gift, which, accepted as a sacred trust, may prove a source of strength and comfort to many."

Touched, but not convinced, as he paused, I asked: "Tell me where and how you live, and what your homes are like? Could

I understand the laws and conditions of your life and growth, it might be easier to believe."

With a tender, half-amused smile, he answered: "If the little children learning their letters in the primary school should ask you to explain to them geometry, astronomy, and physiology, or even ask, as the busy little heads often do, where the babies come from, you could no more make them understand what love and motherhood mean than you could teach them calculus. So you could only tell them to be patient and industrious, to learn thoroughly each day's lessons, to be pure, unselfish, and good, and when they are old enough — that is, when their minds have grown to it — they will understand it all. And so I say to you, my little child, you could not understand me if I told you. As you develop your spiritual nature and come up into this high school, you will find it gradually unfolding to your understanding. We do not come to tell you startling facts or to relieve you of your responsibilities. As your intellect matures and broadens with culture and experience, so will your spiritual faculties expand to greater possibilities of knowledge and usefulness; for all your powers are subject to the same law of growth,—'Use and improve, or abuse and lose.'"

. . . .

Yes, I did receive a letter from you, urging my acceptance of these experiences as veritable truths, without further effort to reason upon them. Unable to accept this as genuine revelation, I have endeavored to ignore and check its workings as much possible; and the subject has become so painful to me, in many ways, that even towards you I have been reticent. But yesterday I was deeply stirred, and it came to me in this wise. I was resting upon the sofa, when suddenly I felt that everything was drifting away from me, and was soon conscious of only cold and darkness. Presently I began to discern glimpses of light, till I could gradually distinguish forms, each clothed in an atmosphere of its own, more or less illuminated by the all-pervading white light. Then I perceived that I alone was surrounded by darkness which the light did not penetrate. Recognizing my father, I asked him if I were dying. He did not reply directly, but after a while said, "Did you not wonder, yesterday, how it would be with you if death were to come suddenly? The light which surrounds and pervades all, is that divine grace which you persist in shutting out of your life. Because you cannot explain to the satisfaction of your small understanding the peculiar conditions of your special temperament, you have closed the windows of your soul and stifled your spirit with doubt."

Then I was made to see my little room in my childhood's home. Around the kneeling form of my girl-self brooded a lovely light; and oh, the face was full of sweetness, trust, and peace! "And now see what we hoped you might become!" Then was revealed to me a far more radiant form, reaching out both hands to men and women, seeming to draw them from a depth of darkness below into the clear light of heaven,—their faces turned to hers, growing peaceful and satisfied as they advanced. "Look well at this picture," he said. "Shall it be a prophecy of your future, or the warning of a lost opportunity? Light is given you; but you cling to darkness, and are wilfully deaf and dumb."

"But how can I be sure, even now, that this is not a freak of morbid imagination, or some brain disturbance?" I said; when immediately it became so dark about me that I could distinguish nothing. Dark and cold as the grave, I began to wonder if I were not really dead and cast into outer darkness. After what seemed a long time,

I thought I saw the flickering of a faint light, which appeared and disappeared, as if thrown back in its efforts to pierce my darkness by a repellent force. It was the light I had seen about my baby; and melted, in an agony of remorse I sank upon my knees, all resistance gone. When I raised my head again, the darkness had so dispersed that I could see my father holding my darling in his arms. He said: "You have fed upon husks and drunk from shallow springs until your soul is famished and wretched. Your peculiar temptation is doubt; it has, and will cost you, many a struggle. When you feel yourself wavering, pray at once with your whole soul for strength, and you will not ask in vain for the grace that renews and invigorates.

"Begin now the eternal life of trustful consecration and sanctified service, consciously drawing your innermost life from God. Life will hold more to you than you have ever dreamed when, ceasing to be an alien, you return to a life of faith, to rest in the conscious nearness and friendship of the Infinite Spirit, knowing that God is not afar off, but nearer than the closest friend, and that nothing is so abiding sure as his love and providential care.

"A gift has been intrusted to you, the value of which you are not capable of estimating. You have now no conception of the work you may accomplish if you are faithful to this trust. But remember your own soul must be illuminated before you can help others; the spring does not brim over with refreshing waters that has not a hidden source. When you have learned, through your soul's deep experience, that the indwelling Spirit is the source of all true living and high service, Nature, which now seems to you a vast machine, will be transfigured into the shining vesture of the Eternal, and the inner chambers of your soul, ever open to the celestial sunrise, shall be filled with its unclouded peace."

I was deeply moved, and wished to pledge myself to a renewed life of earnest seeking and faith; but before I could speak he was gone. Strains of music seemed to float toward me, which gradually died away, and I found myself alive and alone.

"We think that heaven will not shut for evermore
Without a knocker left upon the door,
Lest some belated wanderer should come,
Heart-broken, asking just to be at home;
So that the Father will at last forgive,
And looking on his face that soul shall live.

"We think there will be watchmen through the night,
Lest any, far off, turn them to the light;
That he who loved us into life must be
A Father, infinitely fatherly;
And groping for him, all shall find their way
From outer dark, through twilight, into perfect day."

[The letters of the following eight years have been omitted.]

In passing a certain house during the past year, I have met, almost daily, its former owner. He had been a physician in good practice, and very popular socially, — a welcome guest in many homes. My acquaintance with him was very slight; and feeling irritated at the frequency of these meetings, I usually showed my annoyance by hurrying by without appearing to see him.

These earth-bound souls have it in their power to make themselves very disagreeable if allowed a recognition; and finding this one always there, as much a part of the place as the trees or fence, I began to make *détours* to avoid the neighborhood.

But this zigzag wandering between two direct points was often so inconvenient that from time to time I would venture again on my old direct course, only to find my coming watched for, as before. I mentioned these encounters to M——, in one of our casual talks, as an instance of unpleasant shadowing; but knowing him to have been here exceedingly courteous, she felt he was incapable of intentionally giving annoyance, and urged my speaking.

Thus has come into my life a new experience, perhaps the beginning of a work among these mistaught and erring ones. He told me he had known all along that I had seen him, but would not intrude himself upon me, much as he had hoped to win my interest and sympathy. He was lonely and miserable; yes, he had companionship, but did not care for it; he liked better to roam about his old home and live in his old associations, though it pained him that his wife thought of him as happy in a far-off heaven, and that he could not make her feel his presence. I urged him to leave the earth atmosphere and rise into a higher life, where the stimulus of work is even more urgent than here; but he replied that he could not see what there was for a doctor to do where there were no frail bodies to wear out. He was very much disappointed to find a continued existence so unlike his anticipations, but supposed he must wait for the judgment-day to know whether he was among the lost or the saved. He had always attended church when he could, both from habit and because it was the proper thing to do; but had never thought seriously of religious matters, preferring society and the good things of earth, of which he had an abundance. Nevertheless he had died confessing his faith in the Redeemer. Now things seemed to be turned upside-down; those he had thought unbelievers are so radiant with spiritual light that he cannot endure their presence; while many good church-members are quite the opposite. Then he referred again to the day of judgment, which he seemed to think would adjust matters. I do not think I made any impression upon him in this interview, but we continued our daily visits, and tried to make him understand how all days are judgment-days; that by his own admission he had lived for the physical life alone, and the dwarfing of his spiritual nature is his present judgment; that we are saved by holy lives, not by a vicarious atonement; and that Christ and his true disciples (the Christ-like) are living and working to increase the kingdom of righteousness; and that though he could no longer heal the sick bodies, he could work to save souls. But this idea offended him, — he was not intended to be a minister; and I could not make him feel that in the sense of helping, we are all meant to be ministers.

He never walked beyond the limits of his own grounds (which, however, were quite extensive), yet seemed each day more eager to see us. One Sunday morning we tried to persuade him to accompany us to church, but without avail. Returning, I expressed our disappointment that he had not gone with us, as the sermon and music might both have been a help to him; then proposed his joining us at our evening reading at home, — perhaps too he would like the hymns we are fond of singing. This he would not promise; though I thought I saw a little yielding in his manner, and was not surprised when, later, he came gloomily into the room and took a seat beside me. We gave him no special welcome or notice, but continued the singing, apparently regardless of his presence, for he was evidently much depressed. Before leaving, he thanked me with emotion for the privilege of the evening, adding, "I thought I did not like hymns or sermons, but I find I am just beginning to understand what is meant by spiritual food." The next afternoon he came some distance beyond his place to meet us. I tried to induce him not to go back there; but he would not promise this, although he asked permission to be present again at the reading. Expecting him the following evening, we selected carefully what seemed to us best suited to his mood and need, closing with Whittier's "Answer." He spoke but little, was evidently deeply stirred, and seemed to have taken some strong, silent resolve.

We did not see him the next day, nor the next, but the evening after, as we began the reading, he came among us; and then I knew his determination had been to spare me, if possible, a knowledge of the keen suffering he was enduring.

My father has since told me that it requires great force of will to leave the earth atmosphere, so strong is the clinging to places and associations; and the presence of bright spiritual beings is to these lower ones an almost intolerable pain. The soil and stain of sensual life lies all uncovered in the clear light of the heavenly atmosphere, and it is only through the cleansing touch of this purifying flame that the gathered dross may be consumed, and the spirit regain its Paradise. A free "sanctity of will" remains always and inviolably ours. Help and forgiveness are Heaven's free gifts; but "no force divine can love compel," and step by step we fall or rise, as we will. But our friend was now roused and thoroughly in earnest; he came to us every night, and after a while, for half an hour in the morning. The memory of his past life became more painful to him as he advanced upward, constant in seeking the purifying flame, and so brave and silent about the suffering.

Then there came a Sunday when I was told to be early in my place at church. I found a service, already begun, in that spiritual temple so often unveiled to my sight. At the close of the discourse there was a pause, and he who had finished speaking stood in the chancel, as if waiting, while the congregation remained kneeling with bowed heads.

Presently our Doctor came reverently down the aisle and kneeled before this radiant spirit, who, placing his hands upon the bowed head, looked upward with an indescribable expression of strength and peace. Overcome with emotion, for some moments I was conscious only of the deep silence and of an unusual intensity of white light. Then I heard the exquisite chanting of that heavenly choir; and raising my head, saw our Doctor rise, clothed in his new robe of righteousness, his face so full of peace and victory that I was filled with unspeakable awe.

. . . .

One morning, while busy in my room, a friend from the "Hither Side" asked if he might bring his wife to me; he hoped that I might help her. Having been a hypochondriac for years before her death, she cannot now be persuaded that she is not ill, and clings so to earth that her friends are unable to influence her. Of course I assented, and a little later he brought her, leaving us alone together. She had a weary, discontented face, and the air of one who considered herself injured. I made various unsuccessful attempts to draw her into conversation, receiving only short, cold answers, until the happy thought occurred to me to inquire about her health. It was surprising how she gradually warmed, confiding to me all her ills, and how unjust and unsympathetic she had found her friends there, who wished to persuade her that since quitting the body she was no longer ill. They did not know what it was to be an invalid, and she must cease to expect sympathy. Indeed, she and they seemed to have nothing now in common, and she complained bitterly of loneliness. Oh, if she were only back again in the earth life with her daughter, who had devoted time and strength to her for years! Why had she been so imprudent! She had driven out insufficiently clad, and pneumonia had been the result. I reminded her that her daughter, having spent her youth and strength in devotion to her, needed relief and rest; and hoped that she would soon entirely recover, to be a companion for her husband and bright and well to receive their daughter when she should join them.

She did not give much heed to me, but sighed and looked bored. She was evidently not to be easily moved. The next day I was surprised to see her again, and proposed that she should rest upon my bed. This appeared to please her, and she remained all the afternoon, while I went on with my work, leaving her several times to go down-stairs. I was half amused and much perplexed over this new charge. I dared not offer to read, as I feared nothing more serious than a light novel would be acceptable, nor did I talk much, but tried to make her feel welcome.

The following day she came again, and appeared quite peevish and woe-begone. I was reading aloud, and after a little went on with it. Restless and listless, she soon went away; yet has continued her visits every day since. She seems to like our Doctor, and I believe he will help divert her mind from herself. Her curiosity and interest are apparently excited, although she has no sympathy in our pursuits. Is it not sad? And yet, were she alive (what a singular expression!), finding her so utterly uninteresting and tiresome, I should avoid her as much as possible.

Since this experience I have questioned whether we are right to seek only congenial society. If our sincere desire be to advance the kingdom of righteousness upon the earth, ought we not to give ourselves more freely; to share the culture and refinements that have graced our lives with those less fortunate; and above all, to exert all the influence in our power to win the shallow and selfish to a higher plane of living? My conscience reproaches me that I feel the claim of this weak, selfish, undeveloped woman, as I should not had she been an earthly acquaintance.

. . . .

Last summer, we passed the day with a friend in her old family homestead; and being left alone in the chamber where I had laid my wraps, I sat down in the open window, grateful for a little rest. Dreamily enjoying the peace and beauty of the outlook, I was roused from my reverie by a deep sigh, soon another, and then another, followed, finally, by most passionate sobs. I arose and looked about me; and going to an opposite door, opened it, only to find an adjoining vacant room. I returned to my seat; and distressed by the continued sobbing, was glad to be released from this haunted chamber by the call of my friend a few minutes later.

Returning to the quiet of our home that evening, I asked the meaning of what I had heard; and was told that a brother of our hostess had wished to reach me, but had been completely overcome by the associations of the place. A few days later he came and gave me the sad story of his life, — which is not an uncommon one, I fear. He was the eldest son of a man of rare integrity and purity of character, but of a reserved temperament, much absorbed in his books and profession, and himself so far above the lower temptations of the flesh that this kind of danger to his children did not occur to him. This son was a handsome fellow, genial, warm-hearted, and susceptible to influence, either good or evil. His companions and surroundings were in many ways unfortunate, until gradually he was drawn into the toils of a fascinating, unprincipled married woman. (Oh, the shame of it, that such women are allowed to poison society!)

Later he went to the West; and there, already demoralized, sank still lower, till death suddenly swept him away. And where? Into hell? Yes; but why? What had he in common with pure spiritual souls? That great gulf — the consciousness of sin and unworthiness — had separated him from his parents, who had died some time before, and made him shrink away and hide himself in the companionship of his equals, stifling his conscience in low pleasures.

I cannot tell you what a shock and disappointment it has been to me to find that it is possible to continue a low, depraved life in the world of spirit. I had always thought that the power to sin ended here; but have learned that freedom of choice between good and evil remains as much a law of that life as this, and that there is nothing whatever in death to change a sinner into a saint, except as it brings the sternest judgment, by forcing upon the unclothed soul the exact consciousness of its condition. To the earnest, this is all that is needed to rouse a most ardent desire for the higher life; while to the pure and holy it reveals, to their surprise and joy, the heights they have attained, while, filled with that peace which passeth understanding, they behold the white peaks yet to be attained, rising all fair and glorified in the bright light of heaven.

But though the sinner may descend lower and lower, the saving love is seeking him, and he can find no peace, no escape from that awful conscience which nothing will pacify. No pleasure satisfies, as ever onward he pursues the phantom, till, sated and weary, starving and humble, he comes to himself and bewails the inheritance he has wasted. But oh, how piteous is the return! — step by step, through struggle and atonement, until the lost measure of purity and strength be regained.

I talked with this prodigal a long time, and urged his coming regularly, that we might help and encourage him as we do others; but when I spoke of his parents, it was pitiful to see his shrinking from them and all the sainted ones. How shall I describe to you our anxiety and suffering for him, poor fellow, during the succeeding months of repeated trial and backsliding, while his father and mother directed my efforts and helped sustain my fainting hope? Once, when we thought he had gained a sure hold and was safe, the old dull look of discontent returned, and for days I did not see him. Then our Doctor begged that he might go in search of him and use all his persuasion to bring him back. I was deeply touched, for I felt that he knew that to go into those dark depths was to put himself in the way of old influences and temptations, literally plunging himself into the fire to save another. He left us, saying in his quiet way, without a word of either fear or assurance, "I must go; and if I do not return to-night, you will know why. I only ask that your thought and prayer may go with me." He returned, looking worn and sad; his effort had been in vain. He soon left us; and when he came again the next day, I saw that he was lifted and strengthened, ready to try once more. He was gone several days, — how anxious they were to us! — and this time was successful.

. . . .

One evening, after we had finished reading and were alone, a lovely little girl stood at my knee and most pathetically besought me to find her mamma. I learned that the child had never known earth-life, and that her mother, now dead, was separated from her by a gulf of darkness, — why, she knew not, but had been told that I could help her. I assured her of my hope and desire to bring them together, and she left me with all a child's joy of anticipation.

In the night I was roused by a touch, and saw kneeling by my bedside a young, slight, delicate woman, clad in black and sobbing piteously. I tried to put my hand upon her head; but she shrank away and cowered all in a heap upon the floor, while little by little she poured out her sad confession. Betrayed by her lover, — more sinned against than sinning, — in her alarm and despair she had destroyed the life of her child, and soon after faded away in a quick decline.

She had been brought up under the strictest Orthodox teachings, and believed herself hopelessly lost. Hence the hold he continued to exercise over her when she found him already there before her, through his own reckless act; both doomed, as she thought, and forever shut apart from the pure and good. It would be impossible to portray in words the intensity of feeling shown by these poor sufferers, — their own sense of guilt and degradation, the iron door that shuts them out!

Fortunate it was that I had known something of the man who had wrecked her life. She was not his only victim, — though it was difficult to persuade her of this, for the fascination had been complete; and yet I felt that it loosened his hold upon her.

I said all that I could at that time; and now for many months she has spent hours daily in my room. But my hand trembles and my eyes fill when I recall the dark valley we have travelled together, of which I can give you little idea.

Poor little thing, my heart went out

to her as it has to none other, she was so prostrate and blinded by her sense of guilt, and so drawn by habit of thought and discouragement back to the old life! Many a time she fled from him and from herself to my side, and more than once he followed, pleading or taunting, as his mood might be. Once when in despair for her my soul cried out for help, a quick flash of intense light was the immediate response, from which he fled with a yell like a maniac.

After a while she came to stay most of the time in my room. She was soul-sick, poor child, and lay upon my lounge both day and night; though I often woke to find her kneeling by my bedside. We talked and read a great deal to her, till gradually she came to trust that she could be saved and forgiven, and finally to realize that she still had the power to seek the light which purifies, invigorates, and strengthens.

If hell-fire means anything, — and we are told that every old dogma contains a kernel of truth, — it is this light which purifies as by fire, but which becomes their source of peace and refreshment when cleansed and healed.

Once roused to the full sense of her need, the heroism displayed by our little Lou was sublime. There was no more wavering or flinching, but a patient, resolute determination to regain her lost purity and peace; nor would her conscience be satisfied with less than her utmost endurance. I remember, one day, starting to throw a little white shawl over her black robe, and how she shrank from it, begging me not to put anything white near her. How pleased I was when, long after, she let me spread it over her as she lay on my bed, looking so calm and spent that I wondered how this could be with one set free from the body. But I understand now that the spirit faints and is weary, and have been led to question whether the spirit does not react upon the body here, even more than the body upon the spirit. And then there came a night when she was brought, like one dead, by two shining ones. She did not leave us again for several days, but lay quiet and peaceful upon my lounge, under the little white shawl, with some sprays of sweet white honeysuckle beside her. Upon waking in the morning we found her gone. We knew that this ordeal through which she was passing could not kill, and would not last forever; but oh, how deeply was our sympathy stirred! how interminable seemed those hours!

The next afternoon we were told to be in church at sunset. We found the place filled, the altar exquisitely decked with delicate white flowers, the music enchanting, and the long, deep hush of the worshippers only broken by the soft, low strains. While I listened, awed and breathless, our little charge was borne down the aisle, all spent and unconscious, to the chancel, where one — oh, so bright and beautiful! — waited. He placed his hands tenderly upon her brow; and looking up, seemed to bring down, as in answer, a flood of light ineffable. Every head bowed.

After a prolonged silence, some lovely words were chanted by the congregation. Raising my head, I beheld our little Lou standing erect, her face filled with conscious peace. The little black dress had given place to a robe of pale-blue light, and folded in her arms was her little girl, — the child she thought she had lost forever!

At first I wondered that this should not have been a sacredly private hour; but then I recalled how there is "joy in heaven over every sinner that repenteth," and felt that each soul in that congregation was there from sympathy and joy.

That evening, when my little flock gathered about me, little Lou asked me to read the parable of the prodigal son. I think it had a deeper meaning to us all, as we saw the emotion with which she listened to the story of the son's welcome home to the Father's heart and love.

. . . .

During those months of anxiety over our little Lou, the young man of whom I told you in a previous letter came to me irregularly. Dissatisfied and restless in his old life, yet too weak from long habits of self-indulgence for any continued striving, my time and strength became so overtaxed by his demands upon my sympathy that he was forbidden by my helpers to come to me any more till thoroughly in earnest. This deprivation proved the needed stimulus to his first sincere effort at improvement; for he was a loving fellow, and felt deeply the separation from me and his companions, two of whom had been friends of his boyhood, and were holding to the right more steadfastly than he.

Many days passed before he was allowed to see me, and then I read and talked with him alone, until, after months of slow progress, he was allowed to resume his old place at the readings; and, inspired by little Lou's example, is now one of my safe ones, happy in his awakened sensibility to righteousness, and rejoicing in the loving approval of the father and mother he had so deeply grieved.

The dawn of some interest beyond her own selfish broodings also came to my *invalid* through watching our labor of love over little Lou. My weak ones have always shown a tender sympathy for one another; the slipping back of one is grief to all, while earnest indeed is the joy and pride of each over a brother's hard-won victory. So the unconscious heroism of little Lou stimulated all to greater effort, and won even my invalid from her listless indifference.

"You are queer women," she one day said to me. "Do you really like this work? and is it not a sacrifice to give up society and devote yourselves to such as these?" She has little spirituality, and her progress will be much slower than that of some who have sunk to greater depths.

. . . .

You ask me to tell you more of my "little flock." Many of them have been men of prominence here. That "the first shall be last and the last first," according to the world's standard of wisdom and greatness, is daily illustrated by the humility with which these men of once high places come to learn of spiritual things like little children. Their characters are various, and through devious ways have they come to that "last bourne;" but each separate experience is intensely interesting. I will try to give you fragmentary touches of a few of them.

Dead here to all spiritual life and growth, they have entered the higher life totally unfit for the companionship of the blessed, and in their despair, gloom, and guilt, shrink away from all helpful influences; for only with the soul's cry of Abba, Father! does growth begin.

It has been difficult to understand why this work among the soul-sick and unhappy is given me, when the Better Land is so full of earnest helpers, whose natural and chosen labor would seem to be just here. But we learn that it is less painful for the unspiritual dead to approach one still veiled by this mortal vestment while their sympathies and regrets hold them to earth; but once receptive to wiser teachers, they pass immediately from my guidance into the safe fold.

One who has held my warmest sympathy was here a clergyman, a man of brilliant mind and natural liberal tendencies; but rejecting the higher light, preached dogmas he no longer believed, closing his eyes and understanding to truths inconvenient to accept. His suffering is twofold,—the injury to his own spirit, and a grief yet more intolerable over those misled by his teaching; for he had many enthusiastic admirers, to whom his word and opinion were law.

Two were gentlemen of ample means who lived moral, but narrow, selfish lives, and died leaving their property to public institutions already richly endowed. What would they not give now to be able to relieve the distress of relatives and friends who are suffering from this selfish indifference to their needs! They cannot detach themselves from these lives, following them through anxieties and hardships their care might have averted, so unreconciled at being helpless to aid them, and having only themselves to blame. In some ways these are the most miserable of all who come to me; held back from progress by regrets and remorse, they will not seek for themselves brighter spheres while those they have neglected are toil-worn here.

If people could only know in making their wills what a scourge they may be preparing for themselves, which will one day drive them literally into a hell of regret and unrest, then would charity indeed begin at home and in the community where they have lived, and much misery here and hereafter be spared. Large bequests to public charities will not absolve the soul from a neglect of the modest but pressing needs of those close about him, whom public charities cannot and should not reach, but who struggle bravely and uncomplainingly, doing all in their power to help themselves.

Our wealth, talents, time, culture, and refinements are sacred trusts. The ideal life demands that we give, even as we have received, not from a sense of duty, but as a gracious privilege. Nor will the soul be satisfied with any compromise; it must share its every gift. The purse without sympathy and time and trouble, it may be, is as empty, so far as it has power to grace the giver; while the man who proffers friendship and sympathy, yet does not out of his abundance make that professed interest a substantial help, defrauds his own soul.

Judge C—— was a man of fine intellect and large hospitality, living upon a handsome estate, lord of the domain, and much deferred to in the management of State affairs. His wife had been an Episcopalian, and his children grew up with a preference for that Church. He was not a church-goer himself, loved argument, talked remarkably well, and was always ready for a discussion. Thus slipped along in ease and prosperity a life of sixty odd years, when health began to fail, and the problem of a future life presented itself. His country home was somewhat isolated; and loving intelligent companionship, he invited the Catholic priest, when in that neighborhood, to stay at his house. Religious discussions naturally became frequent and more interesting, with decreasing bodily strength; and a few weeks before his death he was baptized by the friendly priest, absolved from his sins, and persuaded that an acceptance of the Church's conditions of salvation would be a sure passport into happiness and heaven.

He had been years in the spirit-world when brought to me by a dear friend, who had been one of his near ones in earth-life. But oh, the bitter disappointment of this poor soul! He had found a new life, but one utterly unlike that pictured to him by the priest. The teaching of religion was all false, he said; there was no such thing as vicarious atonement, and he did not believe there was a Jesus!

Another was an atheist; a man of large culture, but a reserved, unsympathetic nature, who had thought to solve all life's mysteries by intellectual processes. He was brought to me shrouded in indifference and gloom, "himself his own dark jail," and for months seemed hardly interested in our readings. I wondered, as I watched him pace the floor on the opposite side of the room, so coldly silent, what attracted him to our gatherings. The awakening seemed to come to him during the reading of Dr. James Freeman Clarke's "Apostle Paul;" and through the last pages of "The Legend of Thomas Didymus" he sat with his head bowed in his hands, deeply stirred. The seed was quickened. He had been a man of energy and great strength of will; and once roused to a consciousness of guilt, the swift tide of remorse was terrible to see. A faithless, thankless soul, all his life impervious to the sweet influences of spirit, and finally hurried on his path of recklessness by the fearful crime of self-destruction!

Do you remember the last half of Whittier's "Answer"? It would seem to have been written for these belated ones, and expresses the truth so perfectly that their condition is no arbitrary doom, but the inevitable retribution of a life of sense and unfaith. Nothing that I have read has been more stirring to them than this poem:—

"Though God be good and free be heaven,
No force divine can love compel;
And though the song of sins forgiven
May sound through lowest hell,

"The sweet persuasion of His voice
Respects thy sanctity of will.
He giveth day: thou hast thy choice
To walk in darkness still,

"As one who, turning from the light,
Watches his own gray shadow fall,
Doubting, upon his path of night,
If there be day at all!

"No word of doom may shut thee out,
No wind of wrath may downward whirl,
No swords of fire keep watch about
The open gates of pearl;

"A tenderer light than moon or sun,
Than song of earth a sweeter hymn,
May shine and sound forever on,
And thou be deaf and dim.

"Forever round the Mercy-seat
The guiding lights of Love shall burn;
But what if, habit-bound, thy feet
Shall lack the will to turn?

"What if thine eye refuse to see,
Thine ear of heaven's free welcome fail,
And thou a willing captive be,
Thyself thy own dark jail?

"O doom beyond the saddest guess,
As the long years of God unroll
To make thy dreary selfishness
The prison of a soul!

"To doubt the love that fain would break
The fetters from thy self-bound limb,
And dream that God can thee forsake
As thou forsakest Him!"

Perhaps the most trying of all whom I have sought to aid, is one who here was a man of position and influence both in his church and community, a prominent member of various missionary and tract societies, given to cant, long prayers and graces, strict in his family discipline, rigidly observing every letter of Evangelical religion. He was known to be a shrewd business man, and in consequence of his wide and well-known connection with religious and charitable institutions, became guardian and trustee for many orphans and widows, whom he defrauded of their property, using their means to pursue his growing passion for speculation.

It would be most painful to you, as well as to me, to go into the details of the moral and spiritual degradation of this man, who hid his iniquity under the cloak of righteousness, imposing upon the true and simple by his sanctimonious air and loud professions. He was brought to me by one whom he had wronged, and we have done all in our power to help him; but it has seemed an almost hopeless task to restore to him even a small measure of spiritual life, for there is not a single means of comfort or inspiration to others that does not contain a bitter sting for him. The simplest word of prayer wrings from him a cry of agony. He who prayed so fluently in the prison and reformatory, who was always ready to lead the prayer-meeting or offer the long grace, unable to lisp even the Publican's prayer! He comes with the others, but remains apart, bowed with humility and remorse, unwilling so much as to raise his eyes unto heaven, or even ask that his darkened soul may receive.

I think if there be an unpardonable sin, it is religious insincerity, which seems nearer moral and spiritual death than anything I have seen. A silent sympathy is almost all that I can give to comfort him, together with the assurance that if he will be patient and longsuffering with himself, enduring the healing pain, there shall gradually be restored to him the power to seek forgiveness and the quickening, saving love, in sincerity and truth. For "yet doth he devise means that his banished ones be not expelled from him."

. . . .

The faith in a personal devil and his agents of wickedness was to us a far safer belief than the careless assurance we have grown into, that thoughts and actions are merely the expression of our own uninfluenced individuality. If we remember the number of undeveloped, evil-minded, and malicious souls passing constantly from our midst into the beyond, what more natural field presents itself for the exercise of their wicked propensities than the injury of those here on a higher plane than themselves, and towards whom they seem to feel a peculiar hatred and jealousy? We may be sure that the exact condition of our inner life and spiritual atmosphere is as clear to their vision as are physical forms to our material senses, and that tendencies and moods are open avenues for the influence of these subtle workers to crowd in upon, and by their artful management of vacillating motives ofttimes to turn the wavering balance on the side of wrong and evil. How necessary, then, to keep the mind clear and the heart pure, that good angels may come in and help us to battle out every struggle for right. Presences, good and evil, are ever watching near us; it is for ourselves to determine which shall be the chosen guests of our inner sanctuary.

. . . .

I attended very recently the funeral of a young girl, — an idolized, only child. She was one of my Sunday-school class, and my favorite among them all, — so earnest, and always eager for the best thoughts we could glean for the week's lesson. Her illness had been sudden and sharp; one of those quick snatchings out of the home-life of its very joy and centre. Bereft, and stricken to the very soul, her parents could not be comforted, for "their child was not." The materialistic drift of the father's mind robbed the poor mother of what consolation might have come to her through belief in her darling's gain.

But this faith all unstaid, the great hereafter "only a problematical preacher's tale," hope and trust had no place beside the living reality of crushing sorrow, — an instance only too common of the unfaith with which the beloved of many homes are laid away. Could these mourners but detach themselves from the sway of the physical sense, their spirits, "touched to finer issues," would find the vivid realities of the spirit realm an unfailing source of inspiration and strength.

Can you imagine a more heartrending position than to be in one's own familiar home and place, unseen, unheard, and unfelt, — thrust out, as it were, from the love that has nurtured and blessed us all our lives? So it was with this poor child. She looked about upon the objects of her daily care like one in a troubled dream. There were the plants she had so recently tended, the little singing-bird in the window, the darkened house, her agonized parents, so unconscious of her presence; and then, completely overcome by the hopelessness of comforting them, who thought of her as gone to some distant place, she clung sobbing to her mother in an agony of grief and homesickness. Presently the service for the dead began; and my little friend grew more calm, as sentence after sentence of conviction and hope fell from the lips of our beloved pastor, and at the last allowed herself to be led tenderly away by loving spirits. Soon after, she came to me in my room and begged me to comfort her mother; to tell her that she lived and loved her in the old close way, but could not be happy while she and her father were so sad and unreconciled to her going; that she would like to have stayed with them longer, but was yet with them in thought, love, and often presence, and after so short a time they would have a happier home together in the brighter world.

. . . .

It is always a pleasant thought to me that you hold such an earnest interest in my gift. Yes, it continues with, if possible, more interest than ever; and as "my patients," as you call them, cease to need my help, and pass up into the higher life, they continue to hold their affection for me and to "lend a hand" in this labor of love. But let me begin by answering the questions in your last letter. You ask, "Has this double life, as it were, been a help to you, or an added strain?"

It has indeed been no easy path to climb, thus doubly responsible to those dependent upon me both here and there. If I have sometimes, when discouraged, felt my radiant teachers stern in their exactions, it has been because they would not allow me to rest with less than my best effort. With deep humility and gratitude would I confess their tender patience, always so strong to uplift, comfort, and encourage. They alone know the battles lost or won, and whether at the last I shall be found worthy of so grave a trust and their sustaining help in every hour of need.

What have I found the most impressive fact, aside from the essential spirituality of that life?

It were difficult to select. Perhaps that perfect *order* of the universe which causes every soul to find its own level and exact place, by the same unfailing law that builds the marvellous architecture of snow crystal and flower, and provides for the progress of each soul as surely as for the sweep of the planets on their mighty course. We are just beginning to read in the lessons of nature and history that providential order which we call "law."

We have learned much of the conserving power of Nature; but it remains for the future life to reveal to us that nothing is lost, and that all our toil, study, and self-discipline have been storing the soul with material which, when freed from the fetters of earth, in that life of larger opportunities, will unfold to blessed use. What joy to find what we thought lost in our weary struggle with life saved for us,—stored safely away for future use!

> "He lends not, but gives to the end,
> As he loves to the end. If it seem
> That he draws back a gift, comprehend
> 'Tis to add to it rather,
> Or keep,—as a mother may toys
> Too costly, though given by herself,
> Till the room shall be stiller from noise,
> And the children more fit for such joys
> Kept over their heads on the shelf."

I wish I might say to all mothers who sit with empty arms and aching hearts, that though for a time they may not watch the growth and unfolding of their little ones, yet does their present sorrow enfold unspeakable future joy. When they come to know how their children have been cared for, and led by wise and loving friends into greater possibilities of growth than we can imagine, I am sure the compensations will overpay the heartache of this temporary separation.

And to lives that have here been full of high, pure aspirations, but hedged in by cruel circumstances, what a release does death bring, opening brighter realities than their deepest longings and fairest visions have ever pictured!

Most impressive to the finite mind are also the subtle, far-reaching effects of seemingly small events. The more we realize the perfect order and beneficent purpose of the universe, the more solemn becomes our sense of responsibility; and as reverence deepens into awe, we confess, with the Psalmist of old, "Thou hast beset me behind and before, and laid thine hand upon me. Such knowledge is too wonderful for me; it is high, I cannot attain unto it."

"What do they do, these bright ones?"

I think all that we may know of that higher life is summed up in the teaching of Jesus, — probably all that we can understand of it; certainly all that we *need* to know. First, "Be ye perfect;" and out of that comes the service of the strong to the feeble, "Whosoever will be chief among you, let him be your servant." "It is more blessed to give than to receive." Primarily, it is a life of growth and service.

Do you ask, If, then, we have already

sufficient knowledge of the conditions of a future life, what value has this spiritual intercourse?

First, I answer, we all want to believe in the future life. Does not every added assurance make it appear more probable? If in the providence of God and the development of man we have reached a point where, to certain temperaments at least, "the veil between is taken away," may we not hope that it is perhaps a steadily growing possibility, yet to become an established fact? If I could learn all I might wish of that life; if I could answer any question that I long to know, predict the future, and solve problems through spirit agency, — I should be unable to believe that this experience has any grounds for faith, it would so destroy my reverence and the sense of infinite progress. But what I have been allowed to know seems to be in harmony with the highest, purest revelations of truth which have come to us through the intuition of the great thinkers and seers of all time.

As the world "in the fulness of time" has received new dispensations, I believe that, more and more as we are able to receive it, we shall have continued testimony of the life to come, which shall stimulate our spiritual growth and increase our reverence and humility, emphasizing the truth, "Except ye become as little children ye shall in no wise *enter* therein."

Is it not something to know that our loved ones are living; that if they were true and good, they have their reward in the companionship of radiant souls and in the joys of the higher life; that having here built up the kingdom of heaven within them, they awoke *at home?* And how sweetly solemn is the thought that for the fallen and sin-sick there is such saving power!

Again you ask, "What particular sect seems to be *the* church?"

You will forgive my involuntary smile, though I do not wonder at your question. Verily, I have not received the faintest indication of any sect there. The shining ones have gathered, from all nations and religions, the pure and saintly of the ages, who have feared God, loved their brother, and worked righteousness. The condition there, depends solely upon progress in the spiritual life, without any reference to the helps which have been used.

I have been sitting on the rocks this afternoon. Listening to the stirring harmonies of the ocean and watching the heavy barque laboriously "tacking" against an adverse wind, the steamer plying its steady way, or the luxurious yacht, so slight of build, bending under its overplus of sail, it seemed most fitting that the ocean should have ever symbolized the sea of life, —the promised land stretching away in the unseen distance, the sea, in its interchange of calm and storm, alike to all. The yacht, like the gay life of pleasure and sensuality, may founder, or reach its destination battered and dismantled. The slow and ponderous barque, like the conservative mind with its unwieldy dogmas and long cables of superstition, plodding laboriously against the free winds of Providence, that do not blow out of the *past.* Others, like the steamer, draw a spiritual force from the conserved energies of the ages, using her sails as helps when they can speed her on her way, but depending for steady progress upon the spirit and power which is constantly renewed in the furnace of the heart. And as the ship from year to year is improved in its model and appliances, so the progressive mind receives new inspiration, and its passage is made quicker, happier, and safer by a larger knowledge and improved helps.

There is but one worship, there, and that, the soul's deep sense of need and gratitude, the conscious communion with the Father, in spirit and in truth. Words, symbols, music, are the spirit's tools,—

essential and useful *only* as they serve to build the soul more stately mansions.

To your final question, "Was Jesus God or man? What think ye of Christ?" I answer, I do not *think*, — I know.

As the Egyptian in his reverence spoke not the name of Osiris "lest his name be lightly breathed on earth," so, dear friend, do I falter as I try to speak of him who in the providence of God was the highest and purest revelation of a spiritual soul.

Above the dim mists of superstition and materialism towers this majestic, colossal figure, mantled in holiness, his face all aglow with conscious, intimate communion with the Father, — the ideal sanctified soul. *One* with the Father, because filled with the Holy Spirit; *the* son, because living in the spirit, in harmony with the divine will, — "he hath left us an example that we should follow in his steps." Consider the beautiful spirituality with which he entered the future life; and then, if imagination does not fail you, conceive of a progress of nineteen centuries from that starting-point! Yet is he our elder Brother and our Friend; and enthroned in the loving, grateful hearts of all who have been led by him into a higher life, he lives and works with that great company of holy souls, to lead humanity onward and upward into the perfect light.

It were impossible, with our finite minds and limited powers of comparison outside, or rather inside, the physical, to conceive of the possibilities of progress there. Suffice it for me to say, that having seen such ineffable glory, I know that farther heights are beyond our present comprehension. Merciful it is, that they are veiled from our sight until we grow strong and pure enough to bear them.

www.ingramcontent.com/pod-product-compliance
Lightning Source LLC
Chambersburg PA
CBHW032009010726
47493CB00007B/2336

* 9 7 8 3 3 3 7 2 7 0 3 2 2 *